TITLE

THE PASSION

BY WAQAS ALI

PROLOGUE

Time is a gift that most of us take for granted.

Waqas Ali

Flashback

"Hello four o'clock" the guard shouted from the watchtower,as he glanced through his optics. They were coming and excessively quick to comprehend,what right? was the inquiry everybody had and the appropriate response lay in the personalities of two of the laborers at the mine.These men were Gabriel Salvator and Samson Yankee."They are drawing nearer" hollered the gatekeeper "close the doors !" he added "Ben what it drawing nearer ?" asked a specialist with alarm in his voice "mountain lions close the god damn entryways!" reacted buck with disturbance in his voice."Must we assault?" asked Samson gazing directly toward the traffic coming at them "not simply yet,the foremen should not freeze it will make them obvious objectives for the wolves" reacted Salvator in a definitive way. Salvator was strong medium stature man with a perfectly shaved jaw while Samson was more similar to an outrageous muscle head who kept a long ginger wizard like facial hair. As the men were going to close the entryways the approaching crashes stopped and the residue cleared. There was nothing there, the men started taking a gander at one another in disarray. "Something isn't right" Sam said checking out his companion close to him "The walls!"Salvator hollered as he ran towards the guardians however it was past the point of no return wolves began coming down from the dividers and one battered the gatekeeper before Salvator arrived. This irritated him and he transformed into a dark wolf double the size of a full developed horse,he was enormous and incredibly muscular.The wolves started assaulting the miners,chaos broke and disarray overwhelmed the air. Sam had additionally turned and was killing the wolves that were battering the excavators and was doing as such viciously,he had dark hide with a ginger color on the edges and was the size of a completely mature bull. The wolves they were battling were somewhat more modest than them. The wolf on top of the lookout was a similar size as Sam ,Sal snarled and thundered as he gazed toward the wolf on the lookout. It hopped and Salvator stayed as yet hanging tight for it and when it was near ground he remained on tow and bounced tearing its upper jaw from its lower jaw . It happened so quick the wolf arrived with a missing upper piece of its head , Salvator arrived on the lookout and thundered . Sam tore the wolves that had assaulted them mine appendage to appendage however totally was lost ,every one of the excavators had perished."What have we done ?" asked Sam glancing around at the pieces of tissue on the ground "survived"responded Sal tranquilly yet with misery in his eyes "survive,survive,survive is the thing that we generally do yet they never do Sal" said Sam showing disappointment"we need to accomplish something" he added "no I need to accomplish something , all I need you to do is care for my son" reacted Sal "I can't help disagreeing , we are in the same boat " declined Sam "what benefit is it in the event that he loses us both?" asked Sal investigating Sam's green eyes.Sam stopped for some time then, at that point, gestured in understanding "great I entrust you with my family sibling don't let me down" closed Sal as he turned and strolled towards the door "hello Sal" got down on Sam . Salvator halted and turned his head "endure" said Sam cheerfully. Sal gestured in understanding ,changed and started running towards the gate,he wailed and before long was carefully concealed.

The party

Sky Salvator sat on a wooden armchair with white Samsung headphones on, paying attention to his main tune 'not all legends wear capes' by Owl city from its new collection 'Cinematic'.The tune went:

He doesn't battle wrongdoing

Or then again wear a cape

He doesn't understand minds

Or on the other hand suspend

However, every time my reality needs saving

He's my Superman

A few people don't have faith in saints

Cause they haven't met my father'

He chimed in as he thought back with regards to the occasions he had gone through with his father.His eyes watered and a grin broke all over. It had been a long time since his dad had kicked the bucket at the now deserted mine ,the news had come as incredible dissatisfaction to him and he never figured he would recuperate however they say time mends all injuries and it did. The tune he was paying attention to was the keep going following right after him list and after this he planned to drop by Uncle Sam,s junkyard and chill until the evening.It was his last day of the occasion before he go into his last semester and he was cherishing it."My father is a saint to me" he chimed in denoting the finish of his song.He got up from the seat and gradually strolled to the carport. It took some time for him to choose the method of transport to utilize and finally he decided and took his blue bike and hit the road. Uncle Sam was the nearest Sky got to a dad in light of the fact that even before his dad had passed on Uncle Sam was consistently there for him particularly after his misfortune Sam has taken care of him like his own child. Uncle Sam lived with two of his nephews who are twins Cassius and Callum. Sky rode his bicycle for some time lastly showed up at the junkyard stopped his bicycle at the door and bounced off it. He strolled to gradually checking out the heaps of destroyed vehicles on each side then, at that point, continued further more rapidly. He hit the twist and when he became visible a noisy profound voice said

"Sky my kid how have you been"

"Uncle Sam I missed you how was Brazil?" he reacted with a particularly clear indication of delight in his voice.He strolled further and embraced the huge man who resembled a dad to him.

"Brazil was OK however you realize how lost I can be without you young men" Sam said grinning down at his nephew.

"Sky wasup pick up the pace ,when you are finished playing huggies come and sick show you something" a voice said digging out from a deficit them ,Sky inclined to one side and grinned ,it was Callum his #1 twin. Callum was a tall youthful grown-up with expansive shoulders and a chest brimming with tissue, he had the muscles of a fledgling weight lifter and he had a newly shaved facial hair growth. He and his twin were just about as indistinguishable as two eggs ,one if not cautious can not differentiate among Callum and Cassius.

"alright now don't be desirous Call you can be my huggy amigo too"Sky said unexpectedly

"Gracious extra me the incongruity and move past with it" answered Call grinning

"OK run along now" Sam said peering down at Sky

"Sam you truly don't need to deal with me like a child you know i'm not ten" he said strolling towards Call

"at last you man up to protect your privileges" Call says tossing his arms into the air

"tisk tisk youthful ones ,you entertain me definitely" Sam said as he strolled away.The young men gazed at him as he left and checked out one another laughed,turned and started strolling the other way.

"how old does he at any point think he is?" Sky asked as they strolled

"100 years like he boasts pretty much all the time"replied Call flagging him to follow him

"doubtlessly I implore he lives up to that point" Sky said
"where in the world is Cass?" he added

"uh, I have no clue he left early today discussing some
young lady he met" answered Call "and here we are" he
added pointing at a vehicle covered by a red sheet.

"go on open it" Call said grinning at Sky.Sky saw him then,
at that point, started strolling gradually towards the
vehicle,he held the sheet and stopped then with one
incredible draw he uncovered the vehicle. His eyes were in
a flash loaded up with abundance joy,his face had become
like that of a tasted child candy interestingly. It was his
fantasy vehicle a dark 1966 Shelby 427 Cobra ,it was still as
costly as could be expected and it is basically impossible
that Call could possess this.

"just for you lil sibling" Call said grinning at Sky

"where like whe where di skied" was so overpowered with
satisfaction he was unable to talk appropriately so he was
stopped

"I got it a couple of miles from here there was an auto collision and to my karma I arrived first" he said collapsing his hands taking a gander at the show-stopper "so since I didn't make you anything for your birthday ,here it is cheerful birthday youthful one" he added. Sky froze briefly taking a gander at the vehicle then back at Call

(wow in the event that I come to discover we are connected by blood I wouldn't briefly deny it and how could it be so amazing it doesn't appear as though it was associated with an accident)Sky pondered internally then automatically embraced Call

"uh, buddy this doesn't transform anything i'm not your huggy buddie" Call said delicately getting Sky off him

"thank you kindly" Sky said with such a lot of appreciation

"no sibling thank you for showing me the opposite side of life" Call said being humble "yet Cass is the one you need to thank most he figured out how to get the motor running for the time being" he added as he gave Sky the keys. Sky took them and checked out them in dismay (is this me?) he thought "indeed its you" said Call like he had perused Sky's mind.Sky gazed toward him and grinned again.

"what about we step through it for an examination drive" Sky said as yet checking out Call

"there's a sea shore party a couple of miles from here on the off chance that we" he was stopped by Sky saying

"lets go!".The two got into the vehicle and drove out of the junkyard. Satisfaction was all that filled the environment in the vehicle, the young men planned to have a great time. Sky drove at an exceptionally rapid while Call was occupied with chiming in to Sleep perpetually by Aiden music a renowned musical gang. It took them a couple of hours to show up at the scene and when they showed up Call was sleeping soundly. Sky searched for a pleasant spot to stop his new ride and he thought that it is under a tree near the forest. The sea shore was loaded with youngsters and a couple of moderately aged people,the music there was amazingly boisterous you were unable to try and hear yourself think. There were young ladies in two-pieces all over the place ,it was each man's heaven. Sky sat in the vehicle actually concentrating on his environmental elements then, at that point, delicately tapped Call on the shoulder "awaken" he said

"ok off limits on i'll simply stand by here" answered Call half sleeping and promptly he returned to fantasy land. Sky grimaced (what truly resting at a sea shore party),he opened his entryway and delicately shut it. Grinning and feeling extremely pleased he strolled grandly from his vehicle and he detected a few young ladies murmuring and checking out him. They would check out him a snicker ,he wound his head toward them and took a gander at them then, at that point ,there simply behind them he saw a sight that nearly halted his heart. It seemed like he knew her before conversing with her ,she just stayed there on a stone alone watching the groups ,Sky froze like he had seen a phantom . The young ladies who were seeing him went to perceive what had eaten up his consideration so rapidly and saw who he was taking a gander at ,one the young ladies scowled in disdain and the entire group left leaving a vacant way among Sky and what he told himself was a mermaid. She wore dark tore denim pants and a dark top composed 'Someone Save Me', her hair was dark and streamed down to her shoulders and she wore dark heels. Sky remained there gazing in astonishment (am I seeing effectively) he thought (possibly I should simply discover), as he completed his suspected and was going to move toward her approximately two people appeared suddenly and started shouting at her ,the other person would mark her head.

Seeing this Sky was enraged so he advanced and pushed one the guys ,the guy lost his balance and fell, the girl giggled. The other one seemed a bit older than Sky but they were of the same height "didn't your father teach you to mind your own business kid" the guy said

"who the fuck are you" the other one said standing up

"none of your concern" replied the girl. This enraged the older guy and he tried to slap the girl but sky caught his hand

"didn't your father teach you how to treat women boy" Sky said looking him in the eye

"kid you have some guts well this time your gut is going to cost you" the guy said. He roughly removed his hand from Sky's. Unaware and completely unprepared Sky was given a blow that sent him staggering then stopping, he wiped his mouth blood was already flowing down his nostrils. He quenched his fist and looked up the guy was coming again going for his face, Sky dodged and hit the guy in the stomach sending him on his knees holding his stomach. The other fellow then picked up a piece of wood and charged at Sky but was welcomed by a very powerful blow which sent him crashing back where he had been standing. The blow had not been from Sky it had come from Call who was now standing in front of the guy who was lying on the ground holding his stomach. The girl stared in amazement at the two guys on the ground then at those standing a few meters from her.

"are you okay?"Sky asked the girl.Before she could reply a voice came from behind them saying "not for long" three guys stood there and in the middle was a muscular one with tattoos all over his body. He wore a black vest,black jeans and biker boots.

"who do you think you are beating up my boys like that, of they wanted the girl they should have her" the guy said

"Dog should we get them" asked one of the guys standing with him. The other two guys wore jeans,biker leather jackets and biker boots.

"yes Chester get em" Dog instructed.The two boys took out pocket knives and slowly approached Call and Sky. Sky felt butterflies in his stomach and fear of death overwhelmed him. Call stood there like he did not care and when the two guys got close he moved so fast for a moment it did not seem normal. He broke the arm of the first and knocked him out then held the other one by the neck and lifted him, the guy dropped his knife and had a look of shear terror in his eyes. Dog came from behind and hit Call on the shoulder with a wooden baseball bat and it broke upon impact. Call dropped the boy and slowly turned to Dog . Dog began to back away holding the remains of the bat, to Sky and the girl it seemed as though Dog was staring into the eyes of a beast because his face had turned pale. Call took one step towards him and Dog turned and flee the scene.

"yes run,run like the dog you are" Call said rubbing his shoulder.(pheww what a relief for a moment there i thought he did not feel any pain)Sky thought to himself

"and as for you boys do not test the depth of the river with both feet isn't that right Chester" Call said looking down at Chester who was trembling. "Sky !!" he called out "yes Call" replied Sky

"remind me to see a doctor tomorrow"

"i definitely will" they all turned to the girl,now she was standing dusting herself.

"are you okay" Sky asked once again

"no i should be the one asking that, I'm Jessica Storms" she said extending her hand.

"I'm Sky" he responded smiling then opened his eyes wide "Jessica Storms wait I know you" he added

"Wait wait wait Sky Salvator wow you've grown, its been so long" she said smiling and hugged him.

Revelations

Sky wandered aimlessly in his rest as he was longing for a more sad completion of the episode which hosted happened at the gathering the earlier evening. He could hear from far off that somebody was calling for himself and the voice appeared to get stronger with each turn. Sky gradually woke up and checked out his bedside clock just to acknowledge he was late

"Poop!" he hollered in shock as he hopped of his bed and dashed to his washroom

"Sky!!!" his mother called out from first floor

"I'm coming!" he reacted as he attempted to get his worn-out denim pants on and was likewise attempting to clean his teeth simultaneously.

His mom was simply wrapping up the last egg for the weighty breakfast she had cooked when Sky came hurrying down the steps set out toward the entryway.

"Hold it in that general area!" she hollered checking out him, who was going to contact the door handle

He halted and went to her

"Indeed mother" he said taking a gander at her

"Sky it's the principal day and you didn't shower, how would you even think that Jessica young lady you were rest discussing will like you?" she said with a rough grin all over

"What?! OK quit worrying about we will discuss this when I get back, I love you mother" he said speeding out of the house and pummeling the entryway behind him. He got on his bike and headed out toward the distant horizon.

"That kid will be the demise of me sometime in the future" she said to herself as she found a seat at the table and started eating. She got done and made a beeline for the carport, got her vehicle and headed out toward Sam's junkyard. Shortly she pulled up before the junkyard, it lay there in everything its strength. She gradually escaped her vehicle and saw Sam strolling toward her with great enthusiasm. Hammering the entryway behind her she embraced him and they started strolling into the junkyard.

"What a wonderful little treat Barbra" Sam said focusing on where he was going

"Not really lovely I may address you on that" answered Sky's mom with a tragic face

"Try not to let me know it's with regards to Sky" Sam said as they drew nearer a wooden table encompassed by lush seats. They stayed there and started talking

"Tragically it is, Sam he hasn't given any indication of the change whatsoever" she said in a baffled way

"Point I thought we discussed this, let the kid be he has as of now passed the phase of change, sadly this yet you should simply acknowledge that he isn't a warewolf" Sam said holding her hand

"In any case, Sam"

"No buts Barb no buts" he cut her off

"Right" Mrs Winter said as the alarm to check the start of Math sounded

"Welcome back to your last term at Sunset High" she added and a few understudies cheered and some showed a great deal of energy

"Anyway you will compose a great deal of tests, presently how is that for a downer" she said grinning and the class muttered grievances.

The example continued obviously, very exhausting. Later school Sky and his dear companion Lewis Crownski left in Lewis' vehicle. Lewis said he had something vital to show Sky.. They each snatched a sausage to chomp on, in transit there. They drove for about an hour . Lewis seriously loved quick and enraged so he truly delighted in speeding which consistently landed them in the police headquarters sometimes.

"man I thought Uganda planned to prevent you from careless driving" Sky said gazing eagerly at the street

"no brother it aggravated me ,they have what they call burnouts there and trust me there is something else to life in Africa besides what meets the eye, those individuals partake in a ton" answered Lewis speeding up

"not to think, you used to be unnerved by death as a small child" Sky said ridiculing his companion

"what transformed me is the thing that I will show you amigo" answered Lewis with a more blue demeanor all over, Sky saw and inquired

"Lewis is everything OK?"

"no man, no I'm in extraordinary torment" said Lewis who kept on looking directly to where he was going

"pull over and lets talk" Sky said with interest blended in with dread "try not to stress amigo we are nearly there" answered Lewis as he took a passed on turn and a sign post composed greeting to 'Dim bay memorial park' arose. Instantly the vehicle was driving between graves. Lewis pulled up at one of the stopping regions somewhere down in the burial ground, got out and motioned for Sky to follow. They strolled for a couple of moments with sky thinking about what was happening, who's grave had they come to see. Lewis halted before two graves with immense gravestones. Sky strolled quicker to where his companion was and what he saw made his heart skirt a thump. The gravestones read 'Samantha Crownski and Michael Crownski'. Sky gradually turned his head to take a gander at his companion who just gazed at the grave without feeling all over.

"Lewis I"

"No need, at any rate I accompanied you here on the grounds that I had not welcomed you to the memorial service and I am heartbroken, its only that there wasn't a memorial service I covered them all alone" Lewis said

"what occurred" Sky asked with sparkly eyes brimming with tears

"On our last day in Uganda as we were going to the air terminal, we went through a humble community to top off our vehicle and as we left something began pursuing our vehicle, it was colossal accept me greater than a tiger Sky. My dad drove as quick as possible with an end goal to escape from it however I don't have the foggiest idea how yet it figured out how to hook the vehicle's right back haggle vehicle flipped multiple times before the rooftop ripped off. Through the flipping when the rooftop ripped off every one of us was tossed in various ways. I blacked out and when I woke up I was in the emergency clinic, a man had thought that I'm taken out a couple of meters from the mishap. I asked where my folks were and seeing the appearances on the essences of the specialists I realized everything was lost. The specialists took me to see their bodies and what I saw tore the life out of me, they had been formed to the point of being indistinguishable, I had the option to distinguish them with their matching outfits. I sobbed brother quietly my voice would not come out. At that point a man wearing a dark thin fit suit strolled in, he was around his mid forties. He was the person who had observed me, he inquired as to whether I had any family members I knew and well you realize Sky I don't, really he then, at that point, marked reception papers when I was placed in a shelter and dealt with me. He generally let me that regardless of know he never going to leave me and he stayed faithful to his commitment he won't ever do. He asked where I used to reside and migrated here, he favored I stayed quiet about the passing of my folks and I did, you Sky are the one in particular who realizes they died the remainder of the world thinks I live with my uncle while they live in Britain. So therefore I have been away for just about a year now" he said as he turned and began strolling back to the vehicle

Sky was stunned, he remained there frozen gazing at those two graves of individuals who purchased a vehicle for him on his fifteenth birthday celebration. They were gone very much like that, they were covered secretly.

"come on we should get moving, it's getting dim around here" Lewis called out as he got into the vehicle

The tale of his companion's misfortune got to him such a huge amount to degree that briefly he thought he saw his eyes sparkle purple in the reflection made by the glossy headstone. He strolled to the vehicle and they drove home.

The attack

Sky wandered aimlessly indeed in his rest, he continued making a moaning sound like somebody who was in torment. In his fantasy he was being assaulted by a tremendous monster which seemed as though an alpha product wolf.He checked out the vehicle he was in and in the front sat his closest companion's dad and on the front seat sat the mother.

"Lewis my child whatever happens simply realize we love you OK" the dad said in a delicate dismal voice he sped up "Samantha now!!" the dad hollered as he floated the vehicle.

The mother went after the entryway which was close to Sky and he dropped out falling into the shrubs close by and hit against a tree. As he lay there something with boisterous crashes passed by him in quest for the vehicle. Sky gradually stood up and when he was on his legs he saw a blast in a distance. He started hurrying to where the blast had happened

"Father!! Mom!!"he shouted checking out the disaster area then, at that point, heard snarling behind him. Sky started to turn gradually and there behind the blazes it remained in its monster he shuddered at its sight then it seized him and when it was going to contact him he woke up sitting up. His vision was green then he scoured his eyes and returned them to an ordinary vision.

"Whats continuing?" he asked himself and checked the time it was 06:30 simply the right an ideal opportunity to get ready for school. Sky escaped his covers and ready for school.

"OK for your schoolwork its on page 208" the new science educator shouted as the understudies left the class in a rush.

Sky strolled in the school corridors set out toward the cafeteria, he got in and tracked down an unfilled table to sit in by a corner near the space of the geeks. He then, at that point, gazed at the divider and started doing some profound thought about his fantasy. (It resembled I was remembering what befell Lewis, however how could that be even conceivable?) he pondered internally. He had been indented so somewhere down in his contemplations that he dis not notice somebody find a seat at the table he was at.

"Hello hi hello!!" Jessica wound up shouting

Sky returned to the world and took a gander at her in a shocked way

"How long have you been there?" he inquired

"Adequately long to complete my food and gaze at you for 10 additional minutes, what was on your mind you've been hanging around for north of an hour I was watching you from another table reasoning perhaps you'd notice however ey" she said in a concerned way

"Ohw I'm truly grieved, I didn't know you learnt here" Sky said

"I don't" she answered

"Then, at that point, why are you here?" he inquired

"She is hanging around for me" Trent said sitting on the table and grinning at Jessica

"Uh no I am hanging around for him, I don't know you kid" she said inconsiderately

"Whatever in any case Mr Cloudy who the fuck do you think you are pounding Rick when I was away last term shutting" Trent said now glaring at Sky

"Screw you" Sky offended

Trent stood up and held Sky's collar, Sky liberated himself and spit in Trent's face. It was a go head to head everybody in the cafeteria halted to check out them. Trent cleared the spit off his face and started snarling humble, he gradually extinguished his clench hand. Rick saw it and quickly rushed to stop Trent

"Trent recollect what you are" he murmured to Trent and Sky held Jessica's hand and left the cafeteria. Everybody in there applauded Sky as he left the room. Trent couldn't talk with rage, his eyes became orange and he promptly wore his shades and they left as well.

"Damn it" Trent shouted in rage as he punched an iron post making it twist "that piece of crap I had him" he added talking with such a lot of outrage in his tone

"Trent recall that he is only a kid" Rick said holding Trent's shoulder

"Aaaarrrrrgggg no! I won't take that from him he will pay" Trent said irately leaving his companion. He moved into he vehicle and dashed away.

"What an oddity" Jessica said as Sky drove towards the following town

"Definitely he disturbs me a ton, so what did you say you needed at this particular park?" Sky asked as he took a go to observe a stopping in Colosol park

"You will see stress not" answered Jessica grinning

Sky left the vehicle and Jessica drove the way. She proceeded to sit on a little somewhere down in the recreation area. The recreation area was more similar to a labyrinth and there were individuals there by any means

" do individuals at any point come here?" Sky asked glancing around

"Yea yet you simply don't see them since they are concealed by the labyrinth like plan of this park now cumon stay here" she answered

Sky strolled there and when he was going to sit she stretched out her hands to him

"Care to help me up?" she said respectfully. Sky held her and attempted to pull her up yet she appeared to be weighty then he put more exertion and when she came up she fell on his chest and started kissing him. It astonished Sky briefly yet he continued to react emphatically. His heart started to thump super quick he was unable to trust what was occurring. She at last isolated her lips from Sky's

"Wow what was that for?" Sky asked in astonishment

"Colosol eatery seven o'clock, it's a date" answered Jessica tapping his nose. Sky took a gander at his wrist watch and back at Jessica

"Yet, its generally ten minutes to seven" Sky said

"Then, at that point, we better not be late" Jessica said running back to the vehicle chuckling

"Is this me?" Sky asked himself overpowered with joy.He returned to the vehicle and headed to the café. They had a truly happy time discussing their experiences and Sky acknowledged Jessica was a year in front of him in school yet picked him. He likewise discovered that the folks who were attempting to assault Jessica had thought she was a whore and she had been impolite to them. The date went wel and Sky went with Jessica to her home.

"I truly delighted in Sky you are better than you look"
Jessica said joyfully

"You made my year" Sky said playfully and Jessica
snickered hard

"Owww and interesting too,I love you" she said then gave
him a french kiss "bye see you aound" she added

"I love you as well" he said and they headed out in different
directions.

Sky strolled to his vehicle moving and singing with such a
lot of energy, things had quite recently turned out well for
him for once in his forlorn life. He moved into his vehicle
and drove away at a colossal speed. He paid attention to
Avicii the evenings and chimed in as he sped into the
obscurity. Ignorant he hit something and quickly stopped.
He escaped his vehicle with his heart beating amazingly
quick, he was so apprehensive and asked it was anything
but an individual. He started strolling gradually to the
figure which lay ahead in the murkiness then as he drew
nearer it ended up being a long way from what he expected
there in front of him was a beige wolf with orange eyes
snarling at him. He turned and started running as quick as
he could so he got to his vehicle and escape yet as he was
going to contact the entryway handle it bit him behind his
right foot and ripped off the tissue making blood sprinkle
like it came from a wellspring. Sky tumbled down and
inclined toward his vehicle he was in such a lot of torment
and passing out rapidly. Things started to become hazy and
as they were at their most foggy point he saw the wolf
change into an individual. He was unable to see plainly
everything he could see was a human figure and everything
went dark.

Investigations

"What did that to your child ma'am may be a mountain lion that is as indicated by the sheriff" Doctor Corner said in a delicate voice with an end goal to comfort Sky's mom " I should proceed to take care of different patients don't stress he will be OK" she added and left the scene

Sky's mom turned and checked out her child through the glass mass of his ward

"That ain't no mountain lion" she said with outrage in her tone "however I will discover who did this to my kid" she added with such a lot of fury in her voice, her eyes became light blue and she left the emergency clinic.

The telephone rang a few times yet she heard nothing, it was 2am toward the beginning of the day and Jessica was occupied with making a quick bite for herself simultaneously contemplating her new love life. She had learnt at a similar school with Sky all her and had a preference for him since 2nd grade lastly she had done it he was hers for the long haul. The telephone rang over and over then she at long last heard it and ran higher up to respond to it

"Hi Jessica" Lewis' voice got through the telephone

"Hello who is this?" she asked not ready to perceive what its identity was

"Uh I go by Lewis i'm Sky's dearest companion I observed your telephone number in his telephone"

"Ohw ideal to meet you Lewis, so how may I help you" she cut him before he got done with talking

"Indeed alright I was cutting to the chase, Sky is not doing so well right now at the city clinic" Lewis said in a dismal tone

Jessica heaved for air and dropped the plate she was conveying, it hit the historic upon sway

"What occurred?, no" she asked with a voice loaded up with distress

"A creature assault, says the specialist" Lewis said with a clear tone of incredulity

"Alright thank you for calli uh" she completed her assertion with wails and hung up.

Lewis sat in the seat on the opposite side of the room which looked toward his dearest companion lying there weakly. (Im going to observe who did this to you pal and they will pay the consequences) he contemplated internally gazing at his companion with eyes loaded with rage. He stood up and left the medical clinic. Lewis drove at a high velocity headed home. He showed up got done in a hippy, he came out conveying a dark calfskin folder case and drove farther of town. Later a brief time he was at where Sky was assaulted. The scene was encircled by yellow tapes, the vehicle had not been towed that should have been done in the first part of the day. Lewis took a light from his vehicle and circumvented the vehicle then he tracked down a gouge on the from guard, it had somewhat twist inwards. He inspected that region lastly observed hide got between a collapsed part of the guard. He hauled it out and similarly as he anticipated a creature had done this an extremely uncommon sort of creature. He ran back to his vehicle and took a blue radiation light and started burning the ground where Sky was observed lying oblivious and he saw paws then, at that point, followed them until they went to human feet,(you removed my folks now you need to remove all that I have well that isn't going on) he glared and set back his stuff into the vehicle and headed to a close by fuel station. He got out with his satchel and went into a rest room sooner or later he came out with a long dark coat. Getting into the vehicle he drove farther away from his home and following an hour he stopped before a major chateau. He got out with a little plastic in his grasp which contained the hide. He thumped at the entryway and was allowed in by a fine refined man.

"Lewi my companion how are you?" a cordial however misdirecting voice said from the other assistant of the glass table which sat toward the edge of the little intensely lit room

"Thomas, I really want you to take a gander at this for myself and let me know kind of wolf this" Lewis went directly forthright

The party on the opposite side of the table turned and took a gander at Lewis. He was a diminutive man who shaved yet kept a Hitler sort of mustache. He wore a whit sterile garment which was cut making it hard to see his real garments, he had one those faces one can distrust immediately.

"Alright now whats the issue amigo" he said in a Mexican intonation

"Somebody screwed with who they are not assume to fuck with" answered Lewis in a quiet voice however with proof of smothered fury

"You some abundance tracker presently?" asked Thomas raising one eyebrow

"I don't work for anybody, presently do the tests this is some private issue" answered Lewis

"OK give that to me and follow" Thomas removed the plastic and paced from the room with Lewis right behind him. They got into another room where he put the hide on a scanner and squeezed a blue button to start filtering

"I would prefer not to be the person who got individual with you amigo I feel frustrated about whoever it is" Thomas included a soft tone "Dredd wolf, one of an uncommon animal varieties in these parts I can't help thinking about what its doing here" he closed

"Much thanks to you Thomas I could generally rely on you" Lewis said as he got the plastic with the hide back from Thomas and started leaving

" you know" Thomas said and Lewis halted to tune in

" truly feel frustrated about whoever got on your own side" he closed and Lewis left the house, got into his vehicle and drove back to town. An hour later Lewis had left Barbra pulled up at the scene where her child had been tracked down lying oblivious. She escaped her vehicle and went near the vehicle. She shut her eyes and began taking in air gradually wanting to track down a creature aroma and at last she got it somewhere near the front of the vehicle. She strolled to the guard and her eyes became blue she taken a gander at it and saw a line of hide which Lewis may have not seen and she hauled it out. Sniffing it she knew the specific sort of wolf who had assaulted her child. She grimaced and gradually strolled back to her vehicle, she got in and drove away. She drove for about an hour lastly pulled up before a typical estimated house, it was at 03:30 am in the first part of the day. She got out ,rang the entryway chime and somebody shouted i'm coming from within. She paused lastly the entryway opened up and a person exceptionally indistinguishable from Barbra remained at the entryway he appeared to be amazed

"Spike wha is everything alright" he asked and Barbra answered "no" as she strolled into the house and into the parlor. She sat on the lounge chair near the television and the person followed and sat on the contrary one

" Barbra converse with me, what is alarming your good nature" he inquired

"Boycott somebody assaulted Sky" she said peering down. The appearance all over changed from quiet to furious

"Who?" he asked in a more profound and threatening voice

"It was a Dredd wolf" she answered. Banabus stayed there gazing at the TV which was off and his eyes became a striking shade of blue

"I'll check with my contacts we will see him and make an illustration of him sister" he said and Barbra started wailing. He stood up, sat close to her and embraced her.

"I will see him I guarantee you of that dear sister, he glanced the way of the passageway and his eyes abandoned blue to purple.

"Leave now you have brought disgrace upon us Trent leave you are presently don't part of this pack" an indian elderly person vigorously watched by strong indian men shouted

"I was never a Red wolf in any case" Trent reacted impolitely, diverted his things and strolled

"Susan" the elderly person said

"Grandfather"responded a lovely youthful looking lady most likely in her mid twenties who had light hair

"You should observe this human and kill him before he uncovered us" the elderly person taught

"Indeed grandpa I will" she answered and left the room.

Shocking discoveries

Her heart beat super quick as she hurriedly strolled in the medical clinic set out toward Sky's ward. It expanded rate as she drew nearer, what had befallen him was as yet a secret to her. She took the last turn and there toward the finish of the dim emergency clinic hallway lay her first love inside a ward composed ICU. Tears streamed down her cheeks as she drew nearer and it settled the score more regrettable when she went into the room. She gradually strolled to his bed. His face was alright and his body too however at that point there was an enormous wrap to his left side foot which was at that point absorbed blood. She pulled a seat from the corner and sat close to Sky. Jessica held her sweetheart's hand and delicately put it to her face. She lay on his chest and cried to such an extent. She really lived him with everything that is in her. Ultimately she nodded off on the seat face down. A little ways from the time she showed up Barbra strolled into the ward conveying leafy foods stunned with what she saw, a youngster was sleeping close to her child, Sky had not referenced any young lady in his life. As she strolled to the bed Jessica woke up and cleaned her eyes, they were just about as red as damnation enough proof to show that she was seriously crying

"Hello" Barbra said from the opposite side of the bed in a delicate voice . Jessica gazed upward and reacted

"Great morning Miss Salvator"

Sky's mom took a gander at Jessica for a brief time then, at that point, said grinning

"Jessica, Jessica Storms wow you have grown a ton"

Jessica looked amazed

"You know me?" she inquired

"Ohw yes I do you are the young lady Sky squashed on back in kinder nursery he generally discussed you and your mom was likewise an old buddy of mine" answered Barbra putting the organic products on the counter "are you and Sky a thing now" she restricted her eys in an amicable way

Jessica become flushed "well yea since yesterday" she answered looking external the ward window

"That is the best news I have heard in the beyond about fourteen days" she said "both of you are a generally excellent match" she remarked "well i'm truly sorry your relationship needed to begin an awful note like this" she added now with a dismal face checking out her child

"What occurred?" Jessica asked with tears returning to her eyes

"Creature assault" answered Barbra peering down and when she heard wails took a gander at Jessica. She went to Jessica and embraced her

" Don't cry Sky is a solid kid it will be OK" she said scouring her shoulder

"Tony who the fuck is the Dredd wolf" Banabus said hitting the table hard

"I let you know Ban I don't have a clue about certain folks dressed like the niggas from Matrix additionally came a couple of moments prior posing the normal inquiry and I depend on my two canines I don't know kindly don't hurt me" argued Tony who was a salesman at a little whore shop downtown

"OK fine" Banabus said quieting himself down "if by any possibility you discover tell me" he added giving a card to Tony and left the store.

Tony hung tight for some time then, at that point, gotten his telephone, dialed a number and paused

"Jeffrey talking" a profound voice picked up the telephone

"Uh this is Tony, Tony Sanchez did any of your wolves come to my town?" he inquired

"No why?" answered Jeffrey

"Some child of truly perilous individuals was assaulted here and they are searching for whoever did I and whoever did it is a wolf of your sort" Tony said

"I have no wolves there, stand by noo Trent damn it" Jeffrey shouted "Given proceed to observe Trent right now and bring him home" added Jeffrey actually hollering "thank you Tony I owe you a great deal" he said thanks to him and hung up

Jeffrey scoured his brow thinking about an answer then his telephone rang again and it was from Tony he replied and heard

"Tony you slippery jerk" a recognizable voice said

"No i'm sorry Ban I aaaarrrrrr" Tony didn't complete his assertion as his throat had been torn out of its place. Jeffrey tuned in with sickening apprehension recollecting how he got away from the close horribly experience with Barbra and presently this was her sibling who was supposed to be multiple times more remarkable than her Jeffrey realized he was not going to endure this not to mention have any conspicuous remaining parts

"Presently you pay attention to me Jeffrey your kid has tried the profundity of the waterway with the two feet and you realize what happens when somebody does that, they suffocate i'm coming for you" said Banabus furiously and he hung up.

Jeffrey just gazed at the telephone with sickening dread, he had been grasped with such a lot of dread genuinely his dad had been right when he said Trent was the greatest error he had at any point made. Jeffrey stayed there recalling when his sibling had gotten killed in view of Trent and presently him, no he was not going to allow that to occur. The day passed by very well Banabus let Barbra know what he found and they were going for Jeffrey that evening so they headed to the huge city during the day.Jeffrey lived in a colossal manor which was a couple of miles out of the huge city. The manor was vigorously protected for that evening since they expected company.The chateau was a four story working with 10 gatekeepers at every who were product wolves as well. The front entryway gradually opened and somebody strolled in, every one of the watchmen at that floor turned and checked out the entryway

"Hello folks I go by Lewis and I" here for as a matter of fact Jeffrey" he said grinning

"What is your business with him?" one of the gatekeepers
asked grimacing at him

"I'm here to kill him" Lewis stopped then proceeded "kill
him just so assuming you wold benevolently let me pass
nobody will get injured OK I counsel you pick life" he added

The eyes of the relative multitude of gatekeepers became
orange and Lewis eliminated his jacket and tossed it to the
ground. He wore all dark, at the top he wore a dark short
sleeved T-shirt and on top something like a tactical armor
carrier which effectively facilitated his 60cm samurai edges
which lay intersection each other on his back. He likewise
wore dark armed force pants with a huge belt which needed
to hostlers for his two hotshot guns and down underneath
he wore colossal armed force boots for better grasp on
tricky ground.

"I surmise passing it is" he said taking out the two blades
that were on his back

The two gatekeepers on the left came at him simultaneously
and he hopped up and landed cutting their heads off
simultaneously. One more attempted to paw his face
however he bowed in reverse watching the paw pass right
above him and he cut the entire arm off, the watchman
cried in anguish and he finally let him alone to get some
closure by cutting him through the heart from behind. That
was three down seven to go. The others changed into
wolves what colossal and threatening monsters they were
nevertheless Lewis had seen more terrible. They jumped at
him individually and he butchered them as they came all at
that floor lay dead on the ground making it a slaughter. He
continued further and killed every one of the gatekeepers
on each floor. While he was busy Barbra and Banabus

pulled up before the manor. They kicked out and off for the entryway, they broke it thundering with rage held on just to land in a pool of blood. They glanced around at the dead bodies

"I surmise somebody beat us to the punch" Barbra said

"Ohw please it was not me" somebody groaned and cried higher up

Barbra and Banabus raced to the last floor and as they took a turn they saw Jeffrey running out of a room without an arm draining vigorously, he saw them and tumbled to the ground they checked out the room and somebody showed up cocked and locked blades noticeable all around

"Then, at that point, who screwed assaulted my closest companion Jeff who did it" Lewis said strolling to Jeffrey then he saw that somebody was at the opposite end assuming the corridor he lifted his eyes to see what its identity was and simultaneously Barbra and Banabus hoped to see what its identity was. Lewis and Barbra froze gazing at one another

"What the heck" Lewis moved his lips yet didn't make a sound he was taking a gander at Barbra whose eyes were light blue and hands had 2cm white hooks sufficient proof to show she was a wolf and Barbra then again was checking out the dressing of Lewis and the images on his sword which was sufficient proof that he was a wolf tracker.

Banabus saw Lewis then, at that point, back at his sister and hauled them out of their daze

"You all know one another" he asked and Jeff made a move to get away yet before he got to hop off the floor, Lewis had as of now put a slug in his mind and he tumbled to his passing immediately.

"Miss Salvator" Lewis said in a soft tone

"Ohw vulnerable sweet Lewis Rogers" she said gradually shaking her head "so this is who you truly are" she added

"In the tissue he said returning his weapon into its hostler and his blade in their places

"Uh presentations would be great" Banabus attacked the discussion

"Ohw Ban this is Lewis, Sky's dearest companion marine don't you recall him" Barbra said checking out Ban

"No chance, screw me" Ban reacted checking out Lewis through and through " life has a truly odd method of changing things you have developed" he included awe

"Do your folks realize you do this?" Barbra inquired

Lewis' appearance transformed "they are the motivation behind why I do this" he reacted

"Ohw i'm truly sorry Lewis" Barbra said showing regret

"Is Sky likewise like you?" Lewis asked now checking out Ban

"No the child is a disappointment, he's a sissy" Ban said

"Boycott don't say that regarding my kid he's simply uncommon there's nothing more to it" Barbra said taking a gander at Ban

"Whatever now we realize he has somebody to secure him, see" Ban said checking out Lewis

" He likewise has us" she said

"We won't live perpetually you realize that" Ban said

"I sincerely apologize for meddling in your family second yet please reveal unveil nothing that you have adapted this evening to Sky" Lewis said with his hands in his pocket

"The equivalent goes for you" Barbra said and Lewis squinted his eyes "yes he doesn't have the foggiest idea" she added and his face relaxed

"Alright have a goodnight" Lewis said and hopped off the fourth floor clutched a couple of flights of stairs and he was on the ground in a matter of moments. Barbra and Ban proceeded to watch him go. He got his jacket which was fortunate enough not to get smudged and he wore it. He gazed toward.

Close encounter

"His vitals are ordinary, he will be alright ma'am" the excellent blonde medical attendant said as she left Sky's ward. Jessica sat close to Sky's bed faulting herself for what happened to him(if I had not taken him to my home this would not have happened)she thought she accused herself until she nodded off. A couple of moments after she nodded off Sky woke up and glanced around pondering where he was then the dreams of the earlier night started coming back.(ohwwww so I'm in an emergency clinic extraordinary, me strolling will be a wonder). An hour from that point as he was gazing outside the window Jessica woke up and as she was scouring her eyes he said

"How long have you been staying there?"

"Sky" she said her face illuminating

He turned and saw her grinning

"Face to face"

Tears started streaming down her cheeks and she embraced him and began crying on his chest.

"I thought I had lost you Sky" she said cleaning her tears

"Wow you truly love me this much I thought I was only a pain reliever" Sky remarked

"A pain reliever? No why" she asked in an amazed way

"Anyway perhaps I was a pain reliever for a new heart break you realize something like that" Sky said

"No no i'm not that sort of individual Sky I could never" she said in a soft tone

"Well i'm glad to hear that" he said "ohw there is something i've been importance to ask you" he added

She lifted her eyes to meet his "yes"

"Will you go to the prom with me?"he asked gazing directly at her

She grinned and become flushed "yes I will" she reacted peering down

"Hi Jason" Lewis picked up the telephone with an intense demeanor all over

"Yea definitely Lewi I observed your person man" a voice said from the opposite side

"Who the fuck is it" Lewis asked with such a lot of restlessness in his voice

"Woh stand by chill Lewi my reserve front and center first" the voice said

"Allow me to carry it to you" Lewis reacted

"Nothing no exchange it electronically I don't confide in you tracker fellows" he said incidentally

"Alright whats your record number?"he asked with a ton of bothering in his voice

"Never showed signs of change" Jason reacted

There was an interruption then a signaling sound

"Great his name is … … … … … ." he said postponing

" Jason!!!" Lewis shouted

"Trent Mackolski, Trent" he said "you don't need to be such an ass about it" he added and hung up.

Lewis got up from where he was situated and got his stuff and placed it in his vehicle. He drove off set out toward the medical clinic to see his dearest companion. At the point when he arrived Jessica and Sky's mom were simply leaving and Uncle Sam and the twins were in the ward.

"Honorable men" he said deferentially and they all reacted affably

"Sky pal how can you feel today?" he asked giving his companion a delicate embrace

" incredible bud" answered Sky

"Well we better get moving we need to tow this limousine from the interstate, tipsy rich child once more" Uncle Sam said as they bid their goodbye and left

"So whats for this evening?" Sky asked and Lewis froze briefly

(What does he mean, did his mom tell him?) Lewis pondered internally

"What do you mean bud?" he asked attempting to constrain a grin

"Lewis I know man" Sky said and Lewis' look changed to genuine

"Know what?" he asked not grinning any longer, the air became tense

"That you have a date for prom brother who is she?" Sky said winking at his friend.Lewis' face loose and he started to grin once more

"What are you discussing I don't have the foggiest idea what you are discussing" he cooperated

"Cmon man no mysteries recollect" Sky said grinning and briefly those words got to Lewis since he was keeping an extremely huge mystery from his dearest companion who told him everything except he was simply attempting to ensure his companion

"Alright OK Meredith Hale that is her the one from 1st grade and you I surmise Jess is your date at long last ey bud" Lewis said winking at his companion

"Yea brother i'm so glad man" he said checking out the window

"In any case, brother what might be said about your foot would you be able to walk" he said

"Yea I can the specialist said it was anything but a profound injury however a scratch would you be able to accept that I've been hanging around for three days" Sky said scratching his head

"Indeed brother yes so tell me do you recollect what assaulted you?" Lewis inquired

"Indeed it was a mountain lion" Sky deceived his companion on the grounds that as he was oblivious he had a fantasy of the events of that evening and he saw what precisely assaulted him or who precisely assaulted him

"Are you certain?" Lewis asked with a tone of complete uncertainty and Sky saw that Lewis realized something yet acted ordinary

"Exceptionally certain" he answered

"OK I surmise the Sheriff needs to take care of those mountain lions ey" Lewis said looking external the window with an intense articulation

"Presently leave my sight laborer you disdain me" Sky said impersonating a ruler from of the knight motion pictures they used to look as youthful ones

"Ohw my ruler excuse my smell" Lewis said reacting as the hunchback who was the captive of the lord and bowed leaving the room " see you at school brother" he added entering the hall

Evening came and Sky was released from the emergency clinic and ready for prom. He proceeded to get his date and went to class. The report about his assault had spread and when he strolled into the ball room individuals were stunned how he had the option to walk when it had just been three days. A many individuals gazed and others came to check how he was and he would react obligingly. Lewis then again headed to the rear of the ball room and left his vehicle there and sat on top of a dumpster a couple of meters from the indirect access paying attention to his cherished Avicii playlist when his prey emerged from a dark Mercedes Benz and strolled towards the secondary passage

"Hello Trent" Lewis hollered from where he was. Trent turned and glanced toward him

"What do you need?" Trent asked in a disagreeable tone

"Jeff said hie" Lewis said bouncing off the dumpster arrival on the ground pleasantly then tidied his suit

"You, it was you" Trent said his eyes becoming orange

"No it was you, you are the person who assaulted my pack initial tit for tat" Lewis said taking off his coat and tossing it onto the ground then, at that point, taken out his edges

"You will pay for this" Trent said as he started strolling quick towards Lewis, his suit started to tear as his muscles extended

"Clash of the alphas I like it" Lewis said as he ran towards Trent

Trent thundered and started running as well. He swung left, then, at that point, right, avoided a rushing blow from behind, moved to the right, raised his sword to repel one more assault and figured out how to cut Trent in the paw.Trent held his paw , turned and charged for Lewis once more.They crashed noticeable all around and Lewis gave Trent an amazing kick in the face and Trent squashed hard on the ground. Lewis landed and glanced back at Trent this time he was not grinning or kidding around. Trent got more rankled and started developing his entire suit detached totally and hide began developing on his skin his face started changing it a more canine like face, Lewis could hear bones breaking and transforming then he made a move to strike. He ran and hopped up as he was going to cut Trent's head off he was hit by the rear of Trent's paw and squashed hard into the dumpster. His edges fell in various ways. As he shook his head to recapture center he saw a paw coming for himself and he avoided, it tore the dumpster like a piece of paper briefly he considered what it would have been similar to assuming that was him there. Trent had now changed into an upstanding product wolf an alpha some may call it. It thundered energetically, everybody in the ball room couldn't hear this is a direct result of the music yet Sky heard it and he remembered it from the night he was assaulted. He gave a reason and set

46

out toward the entryway. He hurried to the back and was missed by the dumpster as it passed by him pulverizing one of the vehicles in the parking garage. He stowed away by the corner and peeped. Lewis caught up with avoiding assaults from an alpha product wolf. Lewis got one of his swords and as the monster came for him he slid between its legs and cut its right thigh. It bowed and held its thigh. He turned and betrayed it, the monster thundered in torment .. Sky raced to his vehicle and turned around it. Trent attempted to hit Lewis yet fizzled on the grounds that Lewis turned into the air and arrived before him. Lewis gave him a knee uppercut which made Trent fall in reverse and making the sword sink further into the alpha's body puncturing through the body coming out through the chest. Lewis cleared blood off his face and spat on the ground. Trent's finger marginally moved yet Lewis didn't see it then uninformed Lewis was held by the neck and Trent gradually got to his feet choking Lewis. Trent was threefold the size of a typical person. Trent pressed Lewis' neck so close veins were all around Lewis' face the Trent lifted his avoided hooks going to paw the existence with regards to his enemy when he heard a vehicle horn. He went to see what it was and was hit hard by Sky's vehicle. It sent him pulverizing into the ball divider and Lewis fell into the recreation center close by. Before Trent could recover center he was hit over and over and again until he turned human. Then, at that point, Sky took out a metal base ball bat and hit him hard in the head something like multiple times and took him out. Trent fell face down and lay there still then, at that point, Sky hurried to help his companion. He got him and placed him in the vehicle and switched. Trent started attempting to stand up, he was so enraged. Sky drove away from the ball at an extremely quick speed. Trent changed began for the vehicle. Sky accelerated until the check was at its breaking point, the vehicle went so quick that it would jump a centimeter off the ground every so often. Trent followed energetically lastly acquired on the vehicle ,he mauled it tossing it upwards and it flipped into the air at such a speed it planned to detonate whenever. As it was going to hit the ground somebody got it and slid a couple of meters then, at that point, delicately put it on the ground. Sky lifted his head and saw two individuals a man and a lady dressede in white wearing wolf like masks.His eyes were green as were the lady's as well.

"Who is that?"Sky said in shock

"Escape the vehicle now" the lady said strolling toward Trent. Sky immediately got out and assisted Lewis with exitting the vehicle as well.

"Not really fortunate this time ey youngster" the person said

"I nearly had him" answered Lewis grinning at him which made Sky squint his eyes

"Presently to deal with the wreck you made, leave child assuming you esteem your life" the person shouted as he strolled to where his accomplice was.The monster remained there breathing intensely checking out them

"You have two choices to pick among, life and passing so which is your pick" the lady said without holding back taking a gander at Trent.

The monster thundered a profound satanic thunder and charged for them

They checked out one another and said simultaneously

"Passing it is" they thundered and went for him. They ran in various ways one to the right the other to the left which mistook Trent briefly and before he could wake up from the disarray they were at that point onto him. Giving him incredible blows from their positions . the person then, at that point, gave him an exceptionally incredible blow in the stomach which made Trent need to stoop yet before his knees could hit the ground the lady gave him an uppercut so amazing it sent him into the air ,he squashed down back in his human structure and oblivious.

"Presently to complete this" the person said and started strolling to where Trent lay, he reached an unexpected stop and examined the forest to one side.

Five tremendous wolves leaped out of the shrubberies and handled a couple of meters from him. His eyes became blue and he started to snarl then one of the wolves turned human. He was a strong African american man with next to no hair or facial hair

"Woh we don't need any difficulty we just came for our kid" he said delicately. The person quieted down and answered

"So what do you need here?"

"Coneleas" the lady added

"I just came for my kid that is all and im out of here" he answered pointing at Trent who was unconscious on the tar

"Since when do Bao wolves run with his sort?" asked the person

"Since he came to submit to me as his Alpha and I know what he did to your" he was cut off before he could wrap up

"Try not to burn through my time" the person said

"I am sorry for his sake this won't occur again you have my statement" he said genuinely "the kid bites beyond what he can swallow so may I take him" he added

They remained there gazing at Coneleas . The climate was antagonistic, there was quietness the lady mediated

"Alright you can have your kid however the following time he even considers pulling a trick like this I will end him and your entire pack" she said scowling

"Much obliged to you, cumon young men" Coneleas said and he lifted Trent up and ran into the forest conveying him.

The two heros went to Sky and Lewis

"How did both of you find yourselves mixed up with this?" the person inquired

"Its a tedious account" Lewis said with indications of torment in his voice

"Return home young men and avoid canines they nibble" finished up the fellow and they started leaving. Sky assisted

Lewis with maneuvering into the vehicle and they drove home consistently.

An attack on Sky

Wandering aimlessly in his rest, Lewis moaned and grimaced like he was having a horrible dream. Sky who was alert gazed at his companion who appeared to be losing whatever battle he was having in he universe of the half dead chose to wake his companion. He stood up, strolled to his companion and started delicate shaking him. Lewis opened his eyes like somebody who was going to choke

"quiet little pig the huge terrible wolf won't get you" Sky said prodding his companion

"ohw Sky" Lewis said getting back to the real world

"indeed little pig it is I" answered Sky proceeding with his prodding

"what time is it?" Lewis asked battling to sit up

"its twenty minutes past nine li"

"don't even think about saying little pig" Lewis cut him off

"wow you realize me so well yet it appears I know you not under any condition" Sky said moving from a lively prong to a genuine one.Lewis peered down then at his companion who was currently lying on the contrary sofa gazing at the roof

"I planned to let you know I guarantee" Lewis said contritely

"Lewis you and me are siblings Mon Ami consider the possibility that I had not displayed up the thing planned to happen huh?" Sky said.

"Imagine a scenario in which you kicked the bucket man what do you believe planned to happen to me man, trust is the thing that fortifies a bond my companion" he added before Lewis could answer

"I was attempting to secure you man" Lewis answered in a sorry tone

"Be that as it may, look who ensured who the previous evening?" Sky said

"You ensured me" answered his companion

"Regardless of how solid or talented you are even the most vulnerable or most regrettable individual can save you so don't be hesitant to depend somebody with data on account of somebody's weakness since no one can really tell when they'll have you covered" Sky said as yet gazing at the roof

"Please accept my apologies man i'll tell you all that I know, where should we start?" Lewis said checking out his companion

"That is news for one more day for the present we should zero in on you recuperating... ... .except if obviously you mend" Sky said grinning. Lewis snickered and moaned.

"Wow you were screwed up genuine awful, you can't giggle" he added

"definitely I belittled him and loose" said Lewis squinting his eyes

"him?" Sky said sitting appropriately "how could you realize it was a him?" he inquired

"uh on the grounds that it's a him" answered Lewis somewhat confounded

"did you know who the product wolf was?"

"indeed it was Trent" answered Lewis

"bingo that responds to my inquiry, I have been having dreams of the assault and on one of them the wolf transformed into Trent and I thought perhaps this is on the grounds that I disdain the fellow and my psyche thinks of him as my foe" Sky said now taking a gander at Lewis

"indeed it's him I did a few examinations and arrived at the resolution that it was him who assaulted you" Lewis said gradually standing up

"yet, for what reason would he attempt to kill me I didn't off-base him to that degree" Sky said in a baffled way

"wolves are monsters Sky they are not to be meddled with
by any means even the smallest of incitement can prompt a
slaughter" Lewis said extending himself

"so how long have you been in the..............what are you?"
Sky said

"I'm a tracker a product wolf tracker and I have been doing
this since my folks died in the smash" he answered

"ohw so you discovered that whatever killed your folks was
a wolf" Sky said coming to an obvious conclusion

"Indeed "

"So as a trade-off for my absolution you should work on
something for me" Sky said

"Name it" speculated Lewis

"Stow away, conceal nothing from me once more" he said
grimacing. Lewis' heart skirted a thump before he answered
on the grounds that he had acknowledged there is a great
deal Sky didn't have the foggiest idea.

"Indeed I won't" he answered grinning

"Do you believe his going to be alright?" Barbra said
swallowing down a glass of milk

"For what reason wouldn't he I'm stressed over Jarhead he appeared to be very wouldn't harmed" answered Ban taking a gigantic gnaw off his additional stew wiener

"I didn't get a decent glance at Sky Ban consider the possibility that he's harmed?" cried Barbra

"Quit being such a child Barb the child is alright I seen him" answered Ban unwinding in his seat. Barbra kept eating her eating regimen salad pondering her child, how much risk he was in since he had incited an alpha.

"Nothing will happen to him Barb" Ban consoled his sister and immedietly his landline rang. He got up and responded to it. He talked for around fifteen minutes then, at that point, gotten back with a gloomy appearance all over. Barbra quit eating and checked out her sibling who was never a client of such an articulation.

"What is it?" she asked with dread recognizable in her voice

"Its dad he wants us home right now" answered her twin

"Why?" she asked her appearance turning more genuine

"Salvatore's pack individuals assaulted one of our sanctums so he needs us to proceed to kill those bastards" answered Ban with expanding rage in his voice

"We can't continue to do his awaiting for our entire lives Ban" said Barbra showing uneasiness

"Until we can take on his entire pack there is no way
around it so please lets simply proceed to make it happen
Barb" differ her twin

"What do I tell Sky this time?" she inquired

"Let him know you were sent alright business related poop
and youll be away for some time" answered Ban.

They pressed their stuff and set out toward the air terminal.
Their dad who was the Alpha of all the Eskimo wolves
resided in the north pole, he was a man who prefered to
reside by custom so he libed in a palace which was situated
far into the frosty grounds of Antactica where he segregated
himself from the world. Eskimo wolves known as quite
possibly the most hazardous specie of wolf were
exceptionally uncommon to coincidentally find on the
grounds that the greater part of them were situated at
regions near the Ice palace. A couple were situated in
different locales or nations anyway when their alpha
mentioned their quality nobody would a choose to
disregard that. Coneleus was an exceptionally incredible
and dreaded alpha known for the path of blood he leaves
wherever he went, he was among the warewolves who were
viewed as divine beings due to their achievements. One of
the warewolves who was viewed as a divine being was Sky's
dad, Gabriel Salvatore and his sibling Diaze .These had a
place with a variety known as the dark wolves the alphas of
alphas, destroyers of universes, ripper of spirits and
relatives of Anubis.

While in transit Barbra called Sky and let him know she
needed to leave for some business related stuff and would
have been away for some time.

. . . . .

"I should be separated from everyone else" answered Trent running his fingers through his hair

"What were you thinking I told you not to mind him!" hollered his companion once more

"I said I should be separated from everyone else ggggrrrrrrr" Trent answered standing up now with orange eyes. Rick's eyes became green and he also started to snarl. They stood eye to eye prepared to jump on one another when they were hindered by the senior's child who then, at that point, excused Rick and advised Trent to go to the compound. Around 15 individuals remained in there, they all confronted the course of the pack chief Elder Kai. Senior Kai was a Red Indian red wolf who had acknowledged Trent since he was an Omega Alpha and had made him a player in his pack. He was the person who made the principles that his pack needed to follow and Trent had recently broken one of the significant guidelines, don't allow people to see you change. Trent bombastically strolled to where the senior remained to hear what his discipline would have been. He proceeded to bow before him and quietness won. Senior Kai took a gander at him with disillusionment and Rage then, at that point, started to talk

"Trent you have conflicted with the laws of this pack very ordinarily on the grounds that you need control of your resentment, did I not let you know that your annoyance will be the finish of you?"

Trent gazed toward the senior and started to talk

"Your laws are of no utilization assuming that they let the people menace us like we are a second rate specie"

"You dare argue in such a way to the senior!!" The senior's child said indignantly

"Try not to attempt me Michael we as a whole realize I can bring you down at this very moment" discourteously answered Trent squinting his eyes at the senior's child

"I will condemn, Trent you are here by ousted from this pack leave and stay away forever and assuming that you do return be prepared to confront my fierceness" said the senior. Everybody took a gander at Trent who gradually stood upstanding and scowled at the senior

"You will lament this Kai" Trent said and everybody was stunned when the senior was called out to by him "every one of you notice my words, not all elderly people men are shrewd leave while you actually get the opportunity" he added and started strolling set out toward the compound entryway

"The following time I see you here!" the senior said and was stopped by Trent saying

"The following time you see me here will be your last elderly person"

Trent had left and everybody was excused. There was a great deal of talk concerning how powerless the senior had become since he was disregarded but then he sat idle. Hearing this the senior brought his girl Osoka to his chambers.

"Father you sent for me?" Osoka said as she strolled into her dad's library. Osoka was a thin vigorously bended lady, she had long sparkly dark Indian hair which she integrated with an extremely long pig tail which extended down to her rump. Osoka wearing pants and plain shirts commended by various kinds of laughs. She had an extremely delicate voice which most confused it with shortcoming anyway she was more grounded than she looked

"Indeed I did I really want you to tidy up Trent's wreck" answered her dad in a delicate voice

"How?" she asked squinting her eyes

"The human young men saw Trent so we must choose the option to ... ... .to get him good and gone, so you will take him out" said the senior now in not really set in stone voice

"Indeed father" answered Osoka respectfully.

She had without exception needed to satisfy her dad so whatever he asked she did as a method of making him glad yet this undertaking she had been given was altogether too much her. She quickly left her dad's chambers and went to hers to plan. She changed into dark pants and a dark sleeveless top. Osoka left the compound on her bicycle and set out toward the city where Sky resided. She rode at an extremely high velocity, she had been captured for speeding on many occasions anyway the more the police irritated her the quicker she went. As she drew nearer to town she sped up not really settled and prepared to finish her dad's main goal.

In the mean time Sky had gone out to get a few basic foods since his companion was not in the shape to go anyplace. He escaped the staple shop conveying a great deal of stuff and set out toward his consideration consistently abstaining from dropping anything. He got to his vehicle put the stuff in and as he strolled to the driver's seat he understood that there was a bicycle across the street whose rider appeared to be gazing at him. He got into his vehicle and gradually switched his vehicle and when it was in the street he took off exceptionally quick. This frightened Osoka yet she responded rapidly and followed him. It was quite a pursuit, Sky flawlessly floated at turns like a star racer yet at the same time he was unable to shake off the biker so he thought about an alternate arrangement. He got into the primary roadway and sped until the measure arrived at its breaking point thus did the biker. The speed they were going at one wrong maneuver the car crash would be so muddled not even his mom could remember him. He drove and the biker was drawing nearer and closer then when he thought she was close sufficient he hit the brakes and leaped out of his vehicle into the grass out and about. Osoka,s bicycle hit the vehicle and she was sent flying however exploited it and moved into wolf structure then, at that point, arrival as a highly contrasting wolf. After landing she avoided the vehicle which was setting out toward her, it hit a tree and detonated it a ton of pieces. Sky then again lay there paying attention to his crushed bones going spirit into place, the measure of agony he was feeling there was past anything he had at any point felt for his entire life.As he lay there it hit him, somebody was following him so he gradually stood up and took a gander at the disaster area then a couple of meters from the disaster area stood a wolf gazing at him. It snarled and started coming towards him and it came quick. Sky looked to his in that general area were woods and he set out toward the forest. He was in such a lot of agony his feet were numb however he was all the while utilizing them to escape. The wolf was making up for lost time quick then as the got to a slanted point Sky utilized it as a benefit and sped up yet sadly he was not quick enough. Osoka ripped at Sky's right foot sending him pounding and moving on the slanted land, he moved for around five meters then, at that point, hit against a tree. Osoka stood a couple of meters from Sky hanging tight for him to stand then she would kill him with honor. Sky moaned then utilized the tree to help him as he got up, this entire circumstance was a lot for him making his fury rise. His body started to recuperate quicker and his weighty breathing gradually transformed into a snarl. He gradually lifted his eyes to check out Osoka who was currently snarling, she quit snarling and froze. The female wolf eased back made moves to the back delivering the sound a canine makes assuming it sees something alarming, presently Sky stood upstanding taking a gander at her. She immediately turned and escaped. Sky was stunned with what had simply occurred, he saw his hands to see whether he had paws yet there were none anyway there was a purple light enlightening them. He cleaned his eyes and looked again and the light blurred gradually until there was nothing. He sat down and inclined toward the tree saying thanks to God it was everywhere.

THE END